Genocide Games of Guterres, In a Stormy Time

by Matthew Russell Lee

AF593164

"Secretary General Guterres will be traveling to Beijing for the Winter Olympics."

The United Nations' longtime spokesman Stephane Dujarric slipped it in after ten minutes of reading out press releases to the half dozen correspondents sitting in the 100-seat UN press briefing room.

And no one asked him about it. Qatar state media asked about why the UN escalators weren't working, to get him up the three flights of stairs to Al Jazeera's four large offices (there was, of course, a bank of elevators).

A retired French correspondent who had held a fundraiser with now-convicted global pedophile Ghislaine Maxwell asked a similar question in French. Dujarric, also French and a genocide denier for the UN's Secretary General who less gleefully covered up the Rwanda genocide, answered in French, and smiled.

"No more questions?" Dujarric asked rhetorically, glancing down at the empty mirror of those the UN's media accreditation chief Melissa Fleming allow to ask questions remotely, as nearly every institution in this time of COVID-19, the link of which to Wuhan she spent public money to censor.

Then I leave you in the hands of Paulina Kubiak, Dujarric said. The second spokeswoman in only four months for UN General Assembly President Abdul Shahid of the Maldive, also purchased by China, also going to the Genocide Games. She spoke, without irony, about Shahid calling for an Olympic truce. This while the host was involved in the mass killing and incarceration of Uighurs in Xinjiang, or East Turkestan as many including Kurt Wheelock referred to it. For her, there were no questions at all, not even about the escalator.

It was over. The UN's legitimacy had died long before. But this was a new low, and a new season. And a next text, follow-up to Belt and Roadkill: Genocide Games of Guterres.

From January 21, 2022: Guterres: This visit to the Olympics is not a political visit. We consider that the Olympic Games are an extremely important manifestation in today's world of the possibility of unity, of the possibility of mutual respect, of the possibility of cooperation, of peoples of different cultures, of different religions, of different ethnicities. And this is more important than ever when we see xenophobia, when we see racism, when we see white supremacy, when we see anti-Semitism, when we see anti-Muslim hatred proliferating all over the world... That is the reason why I am going to the Olympic Games. And it has nothing to do with my opinions about the different policies that take place in the People's Republic of China.

Spokesman Dujarric: Okay, sir, I think you're then off the hook.

Will Guterres be taking his Deputy Amina J. Mohammed, supportive of the killing and targeted detentions perpetrated by Buhari of Nigeria? See, Identity Thieves - and, forthcoming, Genocide Games of Guterres. For now, Belt and Roadkill.

Literary Olympics: Genocide Games of Guterres Have Guantanamo Roots and Gulbenkian Foundation Funding - Tale Told From The Inside: http://www.innercitypress.com/literary1genocidegamesicp012422.html

Kurt Wheelock had first heard of the Uighurs in the form of three lost traders, in leather coats, who wandered from East Turkestan into the long arm in the far northeast corner of Afghanistan.

It was right after Nine Eleven. Kurt was living in an abandoned building - one that he was fixing up, he hastened to tell those he now knew - and running an early blog that came after the attack on New York to focus on money laundering and funding of the Taliban.

The three Uighur traders had been grabbed by some self-promoting Afghan ethnic groups and traded to the Americans, like leather jackets, for a best place at the dusty trough of post-Taliban Afghanistan. They had bags put off their heads and were flown, wearing diapers if Kurt remembered it correctly, to Guantanamo Bay to be interrogated. But of course, this time for real, they knew nothing. This took years for the US to admit.

By then Kurt was blogging from inside the UN, reportedly the first blogger there, at least that's how the New York Times put it. Kurt asked the UN about these Uighurs a number of times, mixed in with thousands of smart-ass questions he asked about genocide in Rwanda and then Sri Lanka and then Cameroon and Nigeria - and finally Xinjiang itself, the old East Turkestan.

The UN, to put it lightly, didn't like the questions. Especially about China, and especially by the Chinese sponsored Secretary General, Antonio

Guterres. Kurt exposing Guterres for accepting a golden statue from Cameroon's long-ruling dictator Paul Biya, along with favors in the UN Budget Committee which Cameroon chaired at the time, in exchange for silence on the slaughter of Anglophone had been one thing.

From the UN's point of view, few had heard or cared about the part of Cameroon, Ambazonia some residents insisted on calling it. But China was a bigger deal, with more power over Guterres. To allow an independent blogger to roll out of bed - Kurt did one night sleep in his UN office, hardly the only resident correspondent to have done so but the only one they were gunning for - and take the then-working escalator one story down and ask questions about Chinese genocide was not acceptable. Something would have to be done.

In those days Kurt got along with China's Ambassador to the UN, a genial older man name Li Baodong. The two had spoken at length and became friends of sorts during a UN Security Council trip to Africa, waiting in a long line to board the UN plane in Kinshasa, DR Congo.

Why had Baodong spoken so freely with Kurt? Maybe it was part of his job, part of the approach of an earlier stage of the Chinese Communist Party.

Baodong had represented the CCP in southern Africa, Malawi, Zambia and Zimbabwe, during a time of existential battle with Taiwan. His job had been to get countries to switch diplomatic recognition to the People's Republic of China, away from the Republic of China or Taiwan. This often involved the payment of briefcases of cash to whatever official could effectuate the switch.

Later in the UN, CCP-sponsored hotel magnate Ng Lap Seng would hand paper bags of cash to General Assembly President John Ashe for changes in already-passed GA resolutions, to add in the name of his company the Sun Kyan Ip foundation as the contractor for a casino cum convention center in Macau.

Kurt covered that trial too, for the first time attending every day of a trial down at the Southern District of New York courthouse. Again, the UN had not liked it, and refused to answer on its role. Finally they threw him out of his cushy two-man office, the one he shared with a Brazilian photographer named Luis. It was the beginning of the end.

The next Chinese government briber, Patrick Ho of the China Energy Fund Committee run by Ye Jianming soon to be disappeared by the CCP after giving a diamond to the son of the current US president for a stake in a strategic oil refinery in Louisiana, a Belt and Roadkill special, gave directly to the UN Secretary General and not just the lower profile President of the General Assembly.

Guterres took money from the Gulbenkian Foundation in Lisbon, which was entirely funded by the oil company of a long ago swashbuckler. China Energy Fund Committee, as a way to bribe Guterres and cement China's control over him, over-bid for the oil company. But Guterres, being Guterres, did not disclose the money he took from Gulbenkian. Kurt fastened on this and started asking every day about it in the UN briefing room, before rushing down to the SDNY courthouse for the trial of Patrick Ho, at which more and more UN sleaze was coming out.

By then Li Baodong was no longer China's Ambassador to the UN, having been returned to Beijing for a higher but never too high position in the foreign affairs bureaucracy. There followed a series of new Chinese Ambassadors, each worse than the last at least in terms of Press access. Each, however, had more access to the UN Secretariat through Guterres.

Beyond blocking the access of journalists from Taiwan into the UN, and using the UN Correspondents Association to encourage or enforce silence about China's increasing control of the UN, now the Chinese Mission on 35th Street could tell Guterres and his head of media accreditation Melissa Fleming which journalists to stop calling on. In Kurt's case it went so far as to have him targeted by UN Security guards, pushing out of the UN building once with machine guns. That time they still let him back in the following Monday, thinking that had made their point.

But Kurt insisted on asking about the ouster, again and again on camera. Guterres' lead spokesman Stephane Dujarric said he refused to answer about security matters. His deputy Farhan Haq, a long-standing Chinese government plant from Pakistan, all the way back to when he worked for a supposedly developing world focused faux media still with a big office in the UN, went further. He called Kurt a liar, on camera.

Soon one night when Kurt was covering the pro Guterres and pro China UN Budget machinations down in the basement of conference rooms and the Vienna Cafe, just after he interviewed Paul Biya's Ambassador Tommo Monthe who like Li Baodong before was for some reason friendly with Kurt, they grabbed him. Two UN Security guards forced him to stand up from his laptop on the marble table of the Vienna Cafe, that reminded Kurt of those in an retro ice cream parlor up in Cambridge, Mass; they broke his laptop in the process, a faint echo of what China did to journalists on its own territory and increasingly elsewhere.

As more UN Security swarmed in and UN Budget committee bureaucrats looked on and looked away, they twisted Kurt's arm, literally, and frog marched him out through the UN parking garage, up to the traffic circle and out onto First Avenue. Kurt had blogged about it, from the park across the street from the UN, under the carved sign urging the beating of swords into plowshares.

He had gone to the 17th precinct on 51st Street and asked to file a formal complaint. After a whispered telephone call - to the US State Department Kurt had later found - the police officer had told him that the UN was immune and that nothing could or would be done. They still took down a handwritten complaint, as if to assuage Kurt. But nothing ever came of it, and Guterres, Fleming and Dujarric, with China's plant Farhan

Haq cackling in the back, never let him return to the United Nations.

For months Kurt did his blogging from a bus stop just outside the UN delegates entrance on First Avenue, in the shadow - welcome in that summer sun as Kurt was thrown out in July - of the US Mission to the UN, which never did anything for him. When it got cold that winter, Kurt found another nearby place to run his blog, a public library on 46th Street with free Wifi and electrical outlets for his laptop that now only intermittently would charge its battery.

Kurt would watch UN Security Council proceedings, in which China blocked even lame statements that would have condemned or expressed concern about North Korea, then write stories about them or now tweet them out in real time. He would email in questions to Dujarric and Haq each morning, cc-ing Guterres and Fleming, then watch the UN noon briefing which he had used to dominate. The briefings were shorter now, more like sessions in North Korea. Did Mr. Secretary General have a concern about the killings in Syria. Yes, he did. But not enough to do anything about it.

For a time, as an accommodation to a temporarily concerned UN Special Rapporteur for Freedom of Expression, who soon turned away in Trump Derangement Syndrome landing a tenured professor's job in the process, Dujarric or Haq would periodically email Kurt responses to his questions.

But when he starting asking more about China Energy Committee and other China-related cases he stumbled on in SDNY and now EDNY in Brooklyn which he visited in the afternoons watching the UN noon briefings, even the canned answers from the UN stopped. It was a total freeze out, and China's new Ambassador Zhang blocked Kurt on Twitter, full circle from the days of Li Baodong.

By now Kurt had found a new and better place to work, a cubicle in the front of the SDNY Press Room, next to the PACER terminal and a small fridge and microwave. He covered a dozen cases a day in the SDNY, and some cases across the Brooklyn Bridge in EDNY, not only R.Kelly but also the case of a Chinese spy working in the NYPD to report to the Mission about Tibetan dissidents in Queens. The defendant's name was Angwang and Kurt wrote that story too.

The Chinese Mission, while blocking him, was still watching. Strange things began to happen on his computer, and even to blog posts he post up. Kurt just put up more. And he began, after the Ghislane Maxwell case moved into the stage of possible mistrial due to a Carlyle Group green-lighted juror known as Scotty David, to focus on the Beijing Winter Olympics. Genocide Games of Guterres.

* * *

Kurt Wheelock began by asking questions, as he had all the way back to his days covering housing or the lack of it in the South Bronx. Why were so many buildings abandoned? In this case, why was the United Nations even more hypocritical than usual, when it came to China?

There was more than enough other work to do. Ten days before the Genocide Games, US political clown figure Michael Avenatti had a second trial starting, for stealing the book advance of his then client, porn star Stormy Daniels. It was a quintessentially American case, all about hype and decay and division. Kurt would of course cover it.

But he got to the courthouse late, when already Stormy's literary agent Lucas Janklow was on the stand as the first witness. Kurt dove right in, live tweeting the direct examination by the prosecutors, how Avenatti had repeatedly told Janklow not to tell Stormy anything about money. This went on until the lunch break.

Then Kurt stopped and emailed his questions to UNSG Guterres and his spokespeople, including :

"On SG Guterres' attendance at the upcoming Beijing Winter Olympics a/k/a Genocide Games, please immediately confirm knowledge by the UN of, and SG Guterres' response to, this letter." He linked to a letter by dozens of Uighur and human rights groups. Then he took his laptop out into the courthouse fire stairs to watch the UN noon briefing, to see if his question would get answered.

Things were even worse than usual. Stephane Dujarric came in late and cracked jokes with his state media favorites, from Qatar and Turkey. The Chinese state media, Dujarric treated more solemnly, as if they were diplomats. Dujarric had given a rate questions to Dujarric, only last week, to China Central Television, which had first gotten Guterres to gush about the Genocide Games. Then Guterres had delivered a quote against what CCTV called America's trade war. It was a one-two punch with the UN's flaccid nightstick.

Today there was no mention of the Uighurs' open letter, which concluded "as the highest representative of the UN, your attendance will be seen as credence to China's blatant disregard for international human rights laws and serve to embolden the actions of the Chinese authorities. We therefore urge you to reconsider your decision to attend the 2022 Beijing Winter Games."

Fat chance of that, under Fat Tony. But Spokesman Dujarric did brag that Guterres would leave in the "middle of next week" - February 2? - and would go "to Korea and then taking a plane to Beijing and then flying out commercially out of Beijing." So the plane to Beijing would not be commercial.

Kurt asked, if only to himself: A CCP private jet like UN briber Ng Lap Seng, or Patrick Ho?

Ng Lap Seng, a CCP member from Macau, had been sentenced to four years but then lobbied to get out early due to COVID in the jails. The irony was not lost on Kurt, but the SDNY judge bought into it. There were letters of support from the same rented family members who had attended the trial on SDNY Courtroom 110.

Ng had been released and was immediately flown back to China in a private jet, as the Huawei heiress later would be. Patick Ho upon his release was also quickly spirited away. Ho had been a pro-mainland bigwig in Hong Kong prior to coming to New York to bribe the UN. Now he returned to the reconquered Hong Kong as a hero.

Meanwhile his boss Ye Jianming, who had moved from the diamond to Hunter Biden to being an adviser to the Czech president, was nowhere to be seen, like a certain tennis player. In Xi's China you could just disappear.

In Guterres' UN, they just didn't let you in, and ignored all of your questions. In Kurt's case he was put on the photo array of crazies, to not be let in at any gate even with an invite from a member state. And those were less and less frequent. Guterres and China had gotten the word out. Like a journalist from Taiwan, there would be no entry.

During the Genocide Games, Guterres would be "in the loop" and would, Dujarric said, meet with Xi Jin Ping. No one they let into the UN briefing room asked, Will Guterres bring up Xinjiang? They would just take the canned press releases, like the ones PGA Abdulla Shahid was now sending out via Paulina Kubiak from Bahrain, and run then as news.

Here at the SDNY courthouse things were more chaotic. When the Avenatti trial day ended, with his Federal Defender grilling the literary agent Janklow about his sexist jokes about Stormy-the-stripper, Kurt went out onto Worth Street with the other journalists, to wait for Avenatti's exit.

There were cameramen, both video and still but yes, all male, waiting in front of the courthouse. One of them greeted Kurt and said, Will I ever see you back in the UN noon briefing? It didn't seem like it. Kurt launched a live stream and zeroed in when Avenatti came out, after his three Federal Defenders. The scrum followed Avenatti west to Foley Square, while he talked trash about Michael Cohen.

Kurt asked Avenatti what he'd thought of Janklow's testimony, had it been truthful, how CNN's Anderson Cooper introduced Avenatti to Janklow to strike the book deals. This, Avenatti didn't answer. Perhaps he recognized Kurt from having tried to get his financial affidavit unsealed and partially succeeding. Kurt had then exposed

COVID-relief PPP loans Avenatti was linked to, while he lined up for free lawyers. Avenatti had DM-ed him on Twitter then stopped.

It was another war but one that was fine with Kurt. He turned back into the courthouse and caught the tail end of the trial day in the opioids prosecution of Larry Doud of Rochester Drug Co-operative. It too had a China link, with the fentanyl that China flooded the US with. If this had happened earlier when Kurt was young, when for example he'd snorted heroin for the hell of it in a park in Bushwick, Brooklyn, would he too have OD-ed? Probably. Having life, you had to use it. Kurt wrote a song, Genocide Games of Guterres, and put some open source video with it, two minutes and twenty second, the Twitter maximum at least for his account. Then he uploaded it to YouTube too and quickly got a message that it would be demonetized, as having "inappropriate" content. Inappropriate to whom? #GenocideGamesOfGuterres.

* * * *

As the Genocide Games grew nearer, it supports including the UN's Antonio Guterres grew more brazen. Hours after Kurt had emailed him questions including whether it was a private jet he would be taking, Epstein-style, from Seoul to Beijing, his spokesman rather than answer announced on camera that yes he would be going.

Spokesman Stephane Dujarric added, showing spin or guilty conscience, that Guterres would be returning to New York (and his mansion) on February 6, "a Sunday." Why add that? Other than to try to be able to say, if the Genocide Games opening ceremony was on a Friday, and promoter Guterres would be back in his mansion on a Sunday, he wasn't really missing work?

So was it a personal trip, a personal express of support for mass incarceration and cultural genocide? Dujarric had said that "the Secretary General will be paying, the UN will be paying," for the commercial legs of his trip. So did Guterres think that all UN money was his? Did this explain Dujarric's ghoulish thank-yous for the payment of dues, no matter how small, by countries like Paul Biya's Cameroon and then-narco president Juan Orlando Hernandez' Honduras?

Ironically a week before Guterres left for the Genocide Games his spokesperson said he was watching with concern - always that - the political situation in Honduras. That would be AFTER the narco prez' successor had been chosen, Xiomara Castro, and China had protested the Taiwanese Vice President's stop-over in the US on the way to Tegucigalpa. Now US Vice President Kamala Harris, through an unnamed Senior Administration Office, emphasized that Kamala would not be meeting the VP. Kurt wrote that one up, in a story about what should be JOH's imminent indictment in SDNY.

China understood symbolism, witness its protests of all things Taiwanese. So it the cover up value of Guterres' craven venture to Beijing, by a private jet they paid for just as they'd bid on the oil company of Gubenkian which paid Guterres, was clear.

But not to Guterres' handpicked press corpse. They sat in the briefing room asking about the escalator and why the US was blocking China's take-over of 5G networks. Little mention in this time was the CCP USG of DESA, Mr. Liu, a former Chinese Deputy Ambassador to the UN who was the country's most recent head of the UN's so-called development pillar. Kurt asked about Liu, but there was never any answer. Liu had succeeded another Chinese USG, an old coot directly linked to the crackdown in Tiananmen Square. To Guterres'

UN, like to the Chinese Internet, that had never happened. Kurt reminded himself to put the video of it up, again.

The demonetization by Google of Kurt's music video Genocide Games of Guterres had been reversed on appeal. As Kurt mulled how to announce or update that, he covered Day 2 of the Avenatti trial - in which Avenatti announced that he was firing his lawyers and representing himself. In China the screen would have gone dark, or an opponent of Xi would have disappeared at the slightest hint.

Here, a few years after Avenatti hit the news not for looting a Seattle based coffee chain but for representing a porn star against the president, Avenatti was on his third trial. So far it had gone Loss, Mistrial and now Self-Representation. Kurt live tweeted, while watching and putting up ghoulish video from the UN noon briefing. Dujarric had literally broke out laughing while claiming Guterres was against genocide (on this Day, the Holocaust), and no one they let in said anything. Kurt put it online, along with his stand-up at the UN gate.

When Avenatti was stopped mid-cross of his former office manager Regnier, Kurt again ran out to ask him questions in Foley Square, including whether he would be applying to get US taxpayer money for his own legal representation of himself, at the $850 an hour he bragged he used to charge. Avenatti did not answer; Kurt filmed him all the way across the Square and into 52 Duane Street. Then Kurt ran back to Mulberry, for hot and sour soup and cabbage and pork dumplings. Gastronomy and, yes, the GenocideGamesOfGuterres.

* * * *

Where was the Islamic majority countries, not (only) at the Winter Olympics but relatedly, in criticize China's mass incarceration of the Muslim Uighurs of Xinjiang?

On Day 3 of the Avenatti - Stormy Daniels trial in the SDNY in Manhattan, Kurt was also covering the 1 Malaysia Development Bank case in EDNY across the bridge in Brooklyn. Would Malaysia be sending anyone to the Winter Olympics? Other than the leadership class, which beyond stealing billions with the help of Goldman Sachs were also complicit through silence in the genocide in East Turkestan?

The 1MDB trial, scheduled to start next month before Judge Brodie, was being impacted by COVID, another China connection. First the trial was delayed when counsel tested positive for COVID, as Sarah Palin had here in SDNY, postponing her trial against the New York Times.

Now Judge Brodie announced that if any of the selected jurors was not vaccinated, the juror or jurors would have to sit in the back of the courtroom and therefore there would be no members of the press or public in the courtroom. Kurt tweeted about it, directing it through photo-tagging on Twitter at press freedom groups. Where were they, on the Genocide Games? In Guterres' pocket as usual, functionally. They had said nothing when Guterres had his guards rough Kurt up and thrown him out, and now keep him banned.

In the Avenatti trial things were heating up. Another California consumer hot-shot lawyer, Sean Macias, was the government's witness - after a proffer agreement, of course. It was Macias who porn star Stormy Daniels had approach to sue the former president, the Orange Man, Donald J. Trump. Macias had passed her off onto Avenatti, who he called the hottest lawyer in California, with a $450 million verdict - never paid and so a dead letter - for negligence in connection with Personal Protective Equipment, again with the China echo, at least to Kurt.

Avenatti had paid Macias back with a Cartier watch for the Stormy referral; then Avenatti harassed him on a beautiful September morning - echoes of 9/11/01 - for an immediate $250,000 loan. This was gotten from yet another sharp/k lawyer, Mark Geeragos, who as best Kurt could make out was paid back with a cut of the shakedown case against Nike. Why had Garagos not been indicted for that, as Avenatti had been? These were questions Kurt wanted to dig into. After the GenocideGamesOfGuterres, he told himself. Opposing genocide came first -- except at the UN.

The day's UN noon briefing had been ghoulish, again, with Qatar state media preening even as their Be-In TV channel covered up the negligence of another genocidaire, Paul Biya of Cameroon, in their coverage of the African Cup of Nations in Yaounde. Sports and genocide was the new thing, hotter than NIV payments to college athletes, hotter than the NFL playoff that had just been on NBC like the Olympics would be. Kurt vowed to cover it all. But first the Avenatti. #CourtCaseCast came first, or at least, ran parallel with the #GenocideGamesOfGuterres.

And of course, not to be forgotten, there was #MaximumMaxwell. Finally Judge Nathan had issued an order about the mass sealing Kurt had opposed, for the tenth time, a week ago. The action? She gave the parties another two weeks to explain all of their sealing. A cynic might say it was connected to the confirmation (to the 2d Circuit) process in Washington, soon to be followed with the process for whoever was selected to replace Stephen Breyer. In SDNY, a lawyer from the Federal Defenders, the quasi public firm Avenatti had just fired, was this day pick to be a Magistrate Judge.

Kurt wrote about that one - she had represented a Rwanda genocidaire, not by choice but by assignment, as passionately as a felon in possession charged with putting a gun in a parked car's wheel well on Ogden Avenue in The Bronx - and wondered if writing honestly about judges might soon cause his problems. Another told him that the Federal Defenders had been created to make street criminal defense more well behaved. That due bore digging into, alongside the #GenocideGames. In Malaysia they didn't even have jury trials, Kurt learned. And in China, at least Xinjiang, no trials at all, before you were thrown into a concentration camp. Where were the trial lawyers in this? This was a connection he could explore, like the UN from the outside. #GenocideGamesOfGuterres.

* * **

To blame the Muslim countries for not standing up to China about the Uighurs might be missing the point, Kurt thought. Here in the United States, despite Biden's half-way measure of the diplomatic boycott, not only were corporations like NBC and Mars going all in - the foreign policy intelligentcia were too.

On his way back and forth to the courthouse to cover the Michael Avenatti trial, now in its fourth day, Kurt listened to hipster podcasts like Pod Save the World, in which former Obama officials said Xi Jinping was really impressive and it was time for America to share power.

Was the genocide issue just about power? Kurt put himself in the position of a Uighur, for a moment, subject to being detained and imprisoned for nothing, for stopping drinking - unlikely - or sending out social media messages, more likely.

Kurt was live tweeting the Avenatti trial and now it was heating up. Stormy Daniels herself took the stand, dropping F-bombs about money she had been owed, and her new gig on a TV show about paranormal investigations, in which a doll talked to her.

Avenatti got in only ten minutes of cross examination, and said he'd have six hours tomorrow before a snow storm came. Kurt would have to come in early and type fast. And the Genocide Olympics were only a week ago. How to make an inroad? How to make it stick? #GenocideGamesOfGuterres

* * * *

There was supposed to be a snow storm. In SDNY Judge George B. Daniels had been talking about it for days, in the trial he was presiding over about Rochester Drug Co-op CEO Larry Doud's corporate drug dealing of fentanyl, most of it Chinese. And now Judge Furman in the Avenatti name-checked the storm too, just as he'd mentioned Zoom. Boom!

Meanwhile in Beijing, which had gotten these Winter Olympics, there was no snow. So water resources were taken from the people, many of them locked in so Guterres, whose junkets had already gotten him COVID once, wouldn't get it again amidst his bluewashing of genocide in Xinjiang. Chinese police, if you could call them that, welded people's doors shut. Constitutional rights? Fat change. Fat Tony.

Still now the opening ceremony was only a week away, with Guterres sure to leave before then. PGA Shahid, already selling the UN flag in Bahrain like John Ashe had before him, might be heading straight from there to Beijing, with his ghoulishly named "Presidency of Hope." It sounded like something out of the playbook of Xi Jin Ping, who Ben Rhodes and his Pod Save the World smart alecks praised so effusively. Xi doesn't read talking about like Hu did! Hey, Hitler was a good speaker.

Elsewhcre in the UN, Fat Tony's crony Fabrizio Hochschild was mis-reported by the in house scribes as being fired - but he was still being paid, whistleblowers told Kurt. They gave him a letter signed by a slew of largely also lecherous UN officials, past and present, supporting Hochschild just as Guterres supported Ghislaine Maxwell, and UNSC President - of Hope! - Mona Juul supported Jeffrey Epstein. Among them was Ahmad Fawzi,

Melissa Fleming's predecessor who had spun to Kurt the UN's role in getting his blog removed from Google News. At least that had been reduced.

Now under Tony the UN imitated China. Rather than weld Kurt into his UN office 318, they had thrown him out and tried to erase him. But here he will was. And the snow was coming, if not in Beijing. #GenocideGamesOfGuterres.

* * *

Each morning now when Kurt got to Foley Square he took in front of the court house, on a piece of yellow duct tape a TV crew had left during Maximum Maxwell, a recorded a two minute vlog. The first minute was about the cases - this week, US v. Avenatti, today Stormy Daniels on the cross - and the second minute now about the Genocide Games of Guterres.

Today there was light snow, something there was none of in Beijing. UN correspondents who never asked about the genocide read canned questions off note cards about the environmental issue of diverting water.

On this, Guterres' feckless spokesman Dujarric was willing to deploy an equally canned answer. The Secretary General was always concerned about carbon footprint. Yeah. That's why he was flying to Beijing for days in a closed loop sucking up to dictators, probably by way of Lisbon to visit his Chinese bribe money if not his supposed wife, the Beard Guterres' security called her.

After Kurt finished recording, he got a medium coffee and an everything bagel from the Egyptian guy with a glassed-in cart in front of 60 Foley, and went into the courthouse. The Avenatti trial day still hadn't started, so he had time to upload the vlog, first to YouTube.

But Google's YouTube didn't just say it would take time to check if the video could be monetized, if is was "appropriate for advertisers," as they said. No, they went further and immediately demonetized it. Kurt thought of announcing that on Twitter, but that platform for sale had recently gone further and entirely disappeared then blocked his song about the Burma military coup, supported by not only China but also Guterres. These platforms were falling in line with the Genocide Games. Did they now automatically demonetize or shadow ban anything with the word genocide or Uighurs? Or only from certain, already-flagged channels or accounts?

Avenatti was tearing into Stormy when Kurt started tweeting it. About her paranormal TV show that wasn't even on TV. About the statement she'd put out after getting paid by Michael Cohen, that she never had a sexual relationship with the Orange Man. This she tried to word smith away, that to be grabbed coming out the bathroom and schtumpt was not a relationship.

But what about saying you never took hush money from Trump?

It was from Michael Cohen.

And Cohen was there, telling the courtroom artist whom Kurt knew that he should have worn a T-shirt for this podcast Mea Culpa if he knew he'd be the subject of her drawing that day, that she should get paid less because he like everyone else other than Avenatti and Stormy in their respective plastic boxes.

When it over Kurt ran down to Worth Street with the crew. He started a Twitter Live Video, which the platform immediately mad unviewable. Then he did straight record to phone video of his attempted Q&A. He asked Avenatti what was in the Nike stipulation that he refused to sign - no answer, maybe Kurt could look the Nike version up - then why he had asked Sean Macias if in the last 24 hours he'd taken cocaine or marijuana. No comment.

Finally he got an answer, with what was he thought a softball: Who did Avenatti think should replace Stephen Breyer on the Supreme Court? Avenatti's eyebrows raised above his mask and he answered. Someone young, someone progressive and mostly, a big Democrat.

Kurt ran back and put it on YouTube. And this time, they immediately monetized it. #GenocideGamesOfGuterres.

* * * *

Then there was the story of Peng Shuai. The tennis number one player in the world accused Zhang Gaoli, Chinese vice-premier and member of the Politburo Standing Committee (PSC) of the Chinese Communist Party of longtime #MeToo abuse. In the US, this might give rise to a defamation suit by a men's rights firebrand like one of the ones involved in the #MaximumMaxwell world of Epstein / Ghislaine Maxwell and Prince Andrew.

In China is gave rise to a first threat to disappear Peng Shuai, then a second actual erasure after mentioned it on social media. Gone, all gone, covered up by Guterres' good friend IOC chair Thomas Block.

It was like in the UN, with the cover up of Hochschild's sexual abuse right on Guterres' floor, except that because had yet - yet! see Belt & Roadway - to feel empowered enough by immunity to actually murder his critics, it was only the rough-up and banning routine.

UN erasure, or attempted erasure, in a barrage of publicly-funded platitudes from Melissa Fleming, whom the UNA-USA ghoulishly was about to put on Chinese Zoom to pontificating about all the COVID-19 disinformation. No need to point fingers, unless it was in the eye of journalists she and Big Tony didn't like.

In Bejing the foreign journalists were being threatened not to mention Xinjiang; they were being told about pre-Olympic events late, with the threat of quaranatine looming. The UN's Melissa Fleming was surely on board with this, the use of the spectre of COVID to censor. Guterres' UN and the CCP which bid on Guterres' affiliated

Gulbenian oil company, there were like synchronized skaters.

Even over this last weekend before the Genocide Games of Guterres, the Avenatti case was blowing up, with Judge Furman issuing order after order. First that Avenatti should belatedly file his list of witnesses, then shooting down or delaying most of them. A filing about literary agent Janklow would be sealed, but only until the goverment rested its case, which was coming. Online Avenatti supporters swarmed on Kurt's postings, including the song he had put up, which mostly quoted from the cross examinations, how Stormy Daniels had only called his work like the Sistine Chapel because Avenatti told her too.

A long time Avenatti supporter, who'd previously attacked Kurt for successfully asking Judge Furman to unseal Avenatti's financial affidavit which he gotten him the three Federal Defenders for free, asked, Is this what an unbiased reporter is supposed to do? Kurt brooded on it until the middle of the night when he replied, On the weekends? Yes, with a link his his song GenocideGamesOfGuterres. He's also done a sequel, with a name check of Peng Shuai. It was inexorably moving forward: #GenocideGamesOfGuterres.

* * * *

It was GG minus 4, that is, four days before China's Genocide Games, and Guterres issued a craven video including:

"I thank China and the Chinese people for your commitment to multilateralism and to the United Nations. I count on your continuous support and cooperation... Soon, I will attend the opening of the Beijing Winter Olympics. The Olympic spirit shines as a beacon to human solidarity and I look forward to safe and successful Games. I wish you prosperity in the Year of the Tiger. Xie Xie"

The support Guterres wanted was like China Energy Fund Committee overbidding on the oil company of the Gulbenkian Foundation, payments from which Guterres omitted from his financial disclosures. The mutual prosperity he wished for involved the mutual rip off of African countries and communities: rare earth for China, money fund to siphon for Guterres, both in exchange for supporting long time dictators like Paul Biya and Obiang, et al.

Kurt recorded a piece of the UN video with this phone, with voice over, and put it online. Time was growing short and the collusion of corporate media seem inexorable. Ad with snowboard Shaun White on NBC, Reuters with woke stories about particular athletes, nothing about genocide.

Meanwhile on the Avenatti beat, over the weekend there continued a stream of pleadings and rulings from Judge Furman. Kurt wrote each of them up, and put links to the stories on top of his fast-written Avenatti Sistine Stormy song. Here too there was some shoot back, that an "impartial journalist" should not put out such a song, or only on his personal account.

The song was mostly just quotes from the surreal cross-examination. But Kurt was tempted to reply, Impartial like Anderson Cooper who hooked Avenatti up with the Stormy Daniels bookdeal? Objective like these mounting genocide cover-up stories?

The only way the New York Times covered it, it seemed, was when someone paid big money to take out a paid ad, with the Olympic Circles made of razor wire. Even that the captions was that "The UN" should invoke the Genocide Convention.

Who WAS "the UN"? It was so amorphous as to be meaningless. Of course the UN Security Council would do nothing - China had and has a veto on it. The UN Human Rights Council is a travesty, dictators rubber stamping each others' reports. Not only was Guterres not mentioning the Genocide Convention or genocide - he was bragging about going to the Genocide Games. So began the week leading up to the #GenocideGamesOfGuterres.

* * * *

The spin wars had begun, an Olympics of propaganda. NBC, being questioned in the US Congress about paying Beijing to kill and lock up Uighurs, tried to save face with a segment phoned in not from Xinjiang but Turkey, which itself alternately used the Uighur issue.

Kurt had been in the United Nations when Turkey had used the word genocide in connection with Xinjiang since the Uighurs were, after all, Turkish people. Was the name calling just a form of expansionism? It soon died down. And even then China was getting more and more aggressive in the UN, awaiting it final conquest under Guterres.

When the UN of Ban Ki-moon muttered about the then and now Myanmar military government screwing its citizens after Hurricane Nargis, the Chinese Deputy told Kurt, How is this different than what the US did in Katrina? Or the French doctors who went on vacation while old people died of heat in Paris in August?

Stories were coming out, though: the AI firm iFlytech, adept in tracking Uighurs, would be on Guterres' phone while Big Tony was in the closed loop. For now, looking forward to February 1, Guterres only piece of work was to swear in another American as head of UNICEF. This is how he bought himself out of any criticism by the US, a cheap deal. UN PGA Shahid, it was entirely unclear where he was, between Bahrain and Beijing. Again, no questions were asked of his spokesperson Paulina Kubiak. Money for nothing.

As the Stormy Daniels trial move to end game, Michael Avenatti taking her money was getting harder and harder to defend. Judge Furman ruled that Avenatti could only really get into his "quantum meruit" / how much is my work worth argument if he chose to testify. But then the prosecutors would get to cross examine him, about his conviction in the Nike case and still pending charges in California.

It's not fair, Avenatti essentially said. Kurt didn't have the heart to go chase him in the snow from the courthouse to Federal Defender. Instead he went to the Magistrates Court, best day since the stalking surprise of the Polish-Canadian literary agent. Today he got three cases, one of them a Chinese money laundering case. He NEF-ed that one on PACER, to start getting emailed notice of each twist and turn in the case as he was getting for Avenatti, and would for 1MBD in Brooklyn, even if the press was barred by COVID from being in the courtroom.

COVID testing was looming as one of China's weapons. Any journalist or visitor who raised the Uighur could simply be said to have tested positive for COVID and be made to disappear, for two weeks or longer. Would Guterres be tested? Would he fail, as he had failed the Uighurs and Cameroon's Anglophones, IPOB and the Rohingya? #GenocideGamesOfGuterres.

* * *

Two days before the Genocide Games opened, everything was being done to lightly name check but not focus on them, at least in the US and UN - including by USUN, the US Mission.

Guterres, it was announced at the last minute, would do a stakeout (about Ethiopia, apparently the conflict he thought he could be less blamed for, or the one speaking about which least angered China). Farhan Haq told the friendly room of scribes he had assembled that Guterres would not be taking any questions.

The goal, as usual with Guterres, was to do a rare faux-media hit just before he disappeared on travel, so that the few paying attention would assume he was still at work, and not flying half way around the globe to suck up to genocide.

Predictably, two softball questions were lobbed at his, with one "off topic" question being about Guinea Bissau, a former Portuguese colony that Portuguese colonist Guterres could manage to feign passion about. Nothing about the Genocide Olympics.

But then one of the more cynical of Tony's scribes, from Foreign Policy, came out with a double suck-up. He alleged, with unnamed sources, that the US Ambassador had urged - where? - Guterres not to go to the Genocide Games. Then, as a swipe back, he reported that Guterres said No, he had already angered China by attending some Democracy meeting at which a minister from Taiwan dared to appear.

It did not mention that Guterres blocked all journalists from Taiwan from even entering the UN, and had ordered roughed up and banned the Press which asked about Guterres' omission in disclosures of his link to Chinese bribes. This was the state of UN reporting, in the long run up to the Genocide Games of Guterres.

Bigger picture, a poll came out that most Americans agreed with a boycott of China's Genocide Games - and most of those that didn't, it was because they'd never heard of the boycott. It had been quietly announced in Washington and then drowned out with other rumbling, other faux priorities. It was the ultimate in phoning it in.

If Chaos Under Heaven, which Kurt was reading on his phone on the subway each morning to the now-ending Avenatti / Stormy Daniels trial, was to be believed, both US parties were corrupt on this, at least at the top. Taiwan got sold out; the Uighurs were a bargaining chip. Somewhere in the closed loop Xi and Big Tony were laughing -- socially distanced, perhaps, but laughing.

In the SDNY, Avenatti was no longer laughing. On Friday he had told Kurt that he would be having a beer, and not no comment on his jibe at Sean Macias about coke and pot. By Tuesday, after Judge Furman shot down most of his witnesses and his quantum meruit (how much was the work worth) argument, Avenatti was saying robot-like, I never want to anger you, Your Honor.

This time after live tweeting the charging conference, Kurt ran straight down to Worth Street, and did manage to catch Avenatti coming out. There were fewer print reporters competing for walking questions today, mostly camera people looking for saleable footage of the walking Avenatti. So what to ask him?

There was a strange comment by Judge Furman about a woman in the back row of the courtroom asking about jurors, with a business card that said NYS court and not SDNY. Bizarre, Avenatti said when Kurt asked. After silent walking and no one else asking, Kurt tried a second question, prefacing it with "I hate to ask this, but."

(Later a true believer would call him a sell-out for saying that, or leaving it in the video)

"If you are convicted, do you expect the US Attorney's Office to ask for remand?" Avenatti didn't answer, and Kurt could understand why. Maybe it was ghoulish. Only today he'd also live tweeted, during a lull in the charging conference, a proceeding in which a man in the MDC without legal visits, losing his mind, told an SDNY judge to service his private equipment, "Y'all ain't doin' nothing for me." Some readers thought it was funny, the thread of the years. Others said it was sad, and it was. Kurt didn't label it one way of the other. Call it impartiality, at least on this. It was what it was. GenocideGamesOfGuterres.

* * * *

After UNSG Guterres headed off to Seoul to catch his private jet to the Genocide Games, the criticism came not from in the UN Press Briefing Room, a wasteland of state media zombies, but from the US west coast. Senator Jeff Merkeley of Oregon, one of the few Democrats not automatically dismissive of cryptocurrency, called Guterres "shameful" to going to the Olympics.

Shameless was more like it. Guterres counted on most people not knowing who he was, and most Democrats in Washington supporting him. Marco Rubio had trashed him, too. A bipartisan coalition?

Meanwhile Kurt had RSVP-ed for an online briefing by the UN Office in Vienna, about the 2022 work of the IAEA and corruptos like UNIDO. But they wrote back, "We are not able to give you access." Not able? Kurt wrote a story, and sent a photo of the access-denial email, which could not be forward, to the pro bono law firm Quinn Emanuel. After a few (more) hours of no response, he thought, might they reach out to Merkeley? Liberal to liberal and all?

Avenatti gave his closing argument, getting shut down on the first and last lines, about his father selling hot dogs and himself liking Italian food. Afterward in Foley Square Kurt asked Avenatti if he planned it. No, he said, but tonight I might start with a hotdog and polish it off with Italian food. Last supper, someone online said. #GenocideGamesofGuterres.

* * * *

While Antonio Guterres has slipped off to Beijing, with a fake stakeout about Ethiopia and just ahead of the slam by Senator Jeff Merkely, UN PGA Abdulla Shahid was more openly bragging:

"The President of the UN General Assembly, H.E Abdulla Shahid, will undertake an official visit to China from 3-5 February to attend the XXIV Olympic Winter Games in Beijing. On 4 February, President Shahid will participate in the Olympic torch relay. He will receive the torch from the President of the International Olympic Committee (IOC), Thomas Bach. The President will then take part in the 2022 Winter Olympics Opening Ceremony in Beijing National Stadium. On 5 February, Mr. Shahid will meet with IOC President Bach, followed by a press stakeout. He will then watch events at the Olympic Games."

The Maldives, where Shahid was from, was more openly in the pocket of China than Guterres' Portugal (other than, it seemed, the Gulbenkian Foundation and maybe Guterres' "wife," the set-aside job culture minister of Lisbon who had never moved with him to Geneva, nor now to New York. "The beard," the UN Security guards called her. A code name, of course, like Stormy Daniel's codename by her Dragons when she checked into porn convention hotels).

Kurt wrote up the shameless Shahid story on top of the Merkeley, then headed up to the 8th floor of the courthouse, to see if the Magistrates' Court still had the three older Boricuas now charged with the fentanyl overdose death of ballyhooed Wire actor Michael K. Williams.

On his way Kurt ran into another CJA lawyer, a friend of Michael Randall Long's, who was talking with another lawyer in the hall with its windows looking out on the snowy balcony and Chatham Green beyond it and the Manhattan Bridge.

"How do you like the Avenatti?" the lawyer asked Kurt, phrasing as people did here like a dish in a restaurant, how is the swordfish tonight. Well, Avenatti did like Italian food, even if his jury could not now consider it.

"It's a freak show," Kurt said, slowing down to talk. He got some of his best stories this way. At the UN he used to talk all day, in the halls and then asking questions in the Briefing Room. Here it was more quiet.

The lawyer said she had a good story for him, a Chinese lady she called the prospective client, who wanted to sue China itself. "I don't want to take the case myself," she said, "you know my politics but I was wondering if you might want to write about it, or could think of another lawyer, someone more like yourself than me."

Kurt knew that Michael Randall Long was up to his eyeballs in cases just now.

But maybe he could take this one. Kurt decided to try.

He took down the prospective client's number, said thanks and ran further down the hall, to the elevator to the Mag Court. By the time he got there, the alleged killers of Michael K. Williams had been processed and the doors were locked. So he headed out across Worth Street to the Ali Baba fruit stand, above which was the Law Office of Michael Randall Long. #GenocideGamesOfGuterres.

* * * *

Finally the day came, or days. At 7 in the morning, New York time, the Genocide Games had their opening ceremony in Beijing, complete with stylized movies like the 1936 Olympics. Thomas Bach of the IOC gave a long and empty speech, after white washing the MeToo black out of Peng Shuai. Somewhere in there was Antonio Guterres, his video given out under embargo to the pro-UN scribes, who did nothing with it.

Kurt live tweeted the ceremony, noting that Nigeria had only one athlete at the Winter Games, while even Puerto Rico had two. There was "Chinese Taipei," a made up name for Taiwan. There was Xi Jin Ping in a black glove, raising his hand every so slightly. Then it was time to head down to the SDNY courthouse.

The Avenatti jury had been deliberating for two days. Out on Foley Square Avenatti had explained to Kurt what his father selling hotdogs stories was supposed to convey; the anti Avenatti crowd thought the Q&A was too light. Now it looked like Avenatti might win or at least get a mistrial.

Later morning the jury sent a note, that one of the 12 was refusing to deliberate, going only on emotion. There ensued a fight over what Judge Furman should tell the other 11 - that they could complain again, and maybe get the 12th one bounced and replaced? No, Avenatti said, that would be error. Judge Furman split the difference. Kurt called in to other cases, and his other job.

It was past three o'clock when word of a verdict came in. There were sound problems, and a rush back to the elevator. But both counts came back guilty and soon Avenatti was stone faced leaving the courtroom. He would have to surrender to jail on the West Coast after the weekend.

Kurt asked him, out in the rain, "Federal Defenders, one a scale of one to ten?"

Avenatti stopped and said "Ten." Then stopped again and said "Fifteen." This while Sarah Lawrence College sex cultist Larry Ray was firing his Federal Defenders. At least they had a right to lawyers, and the semblance of due process. It was more than China, and the UN of Guterres, offered. #GenocideGamesOfGuterres.

* * * *

The UN refused to answer Kurt's written questions including about Senator Merkley called Guterres shameful. And none of the scribes they let in asked about it, preferring instead to gush about the return to the wall outside the failing UN Security Council of Guernica - a replica, for course.

But they put this out: "The Secretary-General met with H.E. Mr. Xi Jinping, President of the People's Republic of China, and H.E. Mr. Wang Yi, State Councilor and Foreign Minister, on the margins of the 2022 Winter Olympic Games. He congratulated The People's Republic of China for the organization of the Games and thanked the Chinese authorities for their warm hospitality. The Secretary-General expressed his appreciation for China's strong support to the United Nations" - strong support to Guterres second term, for sure, and bank account, it seemed. Shameful.

* * *

Even as more and more athletes were pushed into quarantine hotels with charred meat and no Internet, the Genocide Games went out, NBC selling cars and soap and insurance and Antony Blinken pumping out statements about female genital mutilation and his upcoming junket to Fiji.

There the Commander, who took power in a coup and then was celebrated for virtual signaling on climate change, was said to be out of the country and sick. No matter. Antony would fly in, even as

Pacific Island ministers phoned it in from their own offices.

Tellingly Papua New Guinea issued a pro-genocide statement cut and paste from the CCP's website, about sovereignty and double standards. In the UN before he was thrown out, Kurt used to prompt Sudan's ambassador Abdel Mahmood to rant about the West's tool box of double standards. Now it was in writing and online and the US' canned statement were hardly distinguishable.

Upcoming at SDNY, now that Avenatti had snatched defeat from the jaws of victory and #The48 continued spiking the football in gifs, was day 3 of Palin versus New York Times. Kurt wrote a song, focused on the Times and not COVID, but it still got immediately demonetized by YouTube. One trial run into the next; the beat was more interesting than the UN but both left genocide UNtouched. Meanwhile Big Tony flew back to New York, his bags jammed with Chinese cash, virtual perhaps. #GenocideGamesOfGuterres.

* * *

In the run-up to the Genocide Games a journalist had been fired by NBC, the story went. Why? Because she was a Uighur. She said NBC had been ordered to fire her by China, the host of the event. The case seemed too perfect, certainly to the decarcelatory Criminal Justice Act lawyer Gul had first approached, and who in turn told Kurt. So Kurt took the tale to another lawyer, his friend Michael Randall Long.

They met in Long's office over the Ali Baba fruit stand, just down Worth Street from the SDNY courthouse. It had snowed and Long's office was cold.

"The windows are old," Long told Kurt apologetically.

"Hey, I'm cold even in the Press Room," Kurt said. It was true. The last few nights as he worked on the PACER terminal, writing up the cases beyond the hype of US v. Avenatti and Sarah Palin v. NYT, he had put on his old suit jacket from defunct Moe Ginsberg that he left hung up in the press room, along with others'.

Kurt told Long what he knew about the case, and Long's answer was typically energetic or naive. "A lawsuit would take a long time," Long said. "I think we might be able to get her job back by taking her up to the United Nations and making some noise. Don't they have a Human Right Commission or something?"

Kurt laughed. "It's called the Human Rights Council, and it's in Geneva. Anyway China has a seat on it, and they pretty much back up dictators all over the world. Hell, they fired a lady I know because she blew the whistle on them giving the names of Chinese dissidents to Beijing. One of them got killed."

Long shook his head. "So the Security Council, then," he said. "They meet in New York, I see 'em sometimes on TV. Aren't they taking about Ukraine these days? And the US is a big player, right?"

"The US has a permanent seat," Kurt said. "But so does China. And Russia, so they haven't accomplished anything on Ukraine if you've noticed."

"I saw something about the Administration bragging about getting a meeting, and then some Ambassadors standing in front of flags with a lady from Norway reading a statement," Long said.

Kurt laughed. "That's Mona Juul, as head of the Security Council. And she refused my questions about taking a loan from Jeffrey Epstein. Like I said, and sang, the UN is corrupt. But be my guest, try to take the case up there. Just, there is no 'We' on this. I can't even get into the building, since Guterres had been in charge. You take her up there, and send a press release how it goes. Only, send me the press release first. A half hour heads up is all I need."

"Sounds like a plan," Long said. They arranged for Gul to come to his office above Ali Baba later in the day, and Long started researching how to get into the UN. He wasn't on the banned list that Kurt was. At least not yet. #GenocideGamesofGuterres.

* * *

File first, ask questions later. That was one of Michael Russell Long's maxims. It made some sense in Federal court, where the right to amend was liberally granted, at least once. But Long had no idea how to file at the UN, or where. So he and Gul headed up to the UN on the 4 train from Foley Square, two stops on the express to Grand Central then four blocks East to the Glass House.

As they walked down the Isaiah stairs on 43rd Street, the 39 floor slab was glinting like a knife in the winter sun. "This UN never did anything for the Uighurs," Gul told him as they passed a felafel truck already firing up for the day. "And in the five years, under this guy from Portugal, and the lady from Chile in Geneva, even worse. But maybe you find the right people."

Long has signed them up for two tourist passes, twenty dollars each. Like a museum, Long had remarked. Or a whorehouse. They waited on line at 46th Street, and flashed the passes when they got to the front of the line.

"Passport?" a guard in white shirt who came over asked.

Long asked, "Why?"

"Only for her," the guard said. "You stay out of it."

"I'm her lawyer," Long said.

"Ooh," the guard said patronizingly. "Wait here." As he walked away the guard muttered, "You must be veeery important."

"Don't worry, Gul, this will just take a minute," Long told her. A man in a suit came back over. He smiled but has a prepared question: "Of which UN member state are you a citizen?" he asked.

"Excuse me?" Long said. He searched his brain for a come-back. "Do you mean if we're from the Cooks Islands we can't come in and look around that, uh, Parliament of man?"

The suited man smiled again. "So," he said, "Taiwan, I take it. Province of China. Chinese Taipei as the IOC puts it."

Gul put her hand on Long's arm. "No, I have a Chinese passport," she said. "It's expired but I have a Chinese passport." They had refused to renew it, at the consulate on 35th Street, when they'd locked her parents up in a concentration camp outside Urumqi.

"Then how did you fly here?" the suited man asked.

"I live here," Gul said. "I have a work visa." She paused. "I'm a refugee. The UN is supposed to help me."

Someone, another guard it seemed, laughed. "Not necessarily," the suited man said. #GenocideGamesOfGuterres.

* * *

In the run-up to the Genocide Games, not only did UNSG Guterres brag about going to the opening ceremony in honor of, what else, diversity (he had a disability of conscience, of course). In Geneva, his hand picked fellow corrupto Michele Bachelet personally put the kibosh on a report about the concentration camps in Xinjiang.

This came after Bachelet and Guterres had hauled off and fired staffer Emma Reilly, who had gone public with the UN passing the names of Uighurs who signed up to speak in Geneva to the CCP in China, which killed at least one of them.

Kurt had written about that, and drawn a condemnation online from Bachelet's hatchet man Rupert Colville. Like Kurt, Reilly had tried to put her name in the ring to run for UNSG in 2021. But both had their letters and c.v.'s blocked by the Turk in charge at the time, Volkan Bozkir, at the direction of Guterres. This was consist with Bozkir's real boss' abandonment of the Uighurs after 2009.

In January 2022 the UN Security Council was presided over by Mona Juul of Norway. Her husband Terje Roed Larsen had taken a personal loan for $130,000 from convicted global pedophile Jeffrey Epstein. Epstein had also paid $150,000 to take the "UN community" to a showing of a Broadway play about Juul's and Larsen's work on the Olso Accords. Like most Broadway plays, this was was pure fiction - in this case, paid for by a pedophile.

Now Juul and her staff at the mission of Norway, set to grab many members for lack of principle in Beijing, refused to answer Kurt's written questions about the Epstein loan, and anything else, not only the Uighurs but also the Anglophones of Cameroon, and Nnamdi Kanu imprisoned by Nigeria.

There is a journalist name Guchehra Hoja, more on whom in future Inner City Press bonus editions. #GenocideGamesOfGuterres.

* * * *

As Michael Randall Long and Gul waited to the side while tourists entered the UN with their twenty dollar ticket, he texted Kurt to ask him what do it. It wasn't the arms-length press release that Kurt had asked for but it would have to do for now.

"Ask to see Paulo de Souza," Kurt texted back. "And if that doesn't work, ask for Courtenay

Rattray." The Rat Man was Guterres' new chief of staff, replacing the play-out former Brazil Ambassador Guterres had used in his first term. Rattaray had blocked Kurt on Twitter even before Guterres had him thrown out of the UN.

When the suited man came back, and before he could order Long and Gul out of the UN's campus, Long dropped the name. "I'm a lawyer and I'm here to see Paulo de Souza," he announced. "If he is not available, then Courtenay Rattray."

The suited man smirked but a little less surely. "Do you have an appointment?"

"It's a legal matter which would put the Secretary General in an uncomfortable position," Long ad-libbed. Then he deployed what Kurt had said could be a code-word. "Tell them it concerns the Gulbenkian Foundation."

The suited man shrugged and again retreated. "What's that?" Gul asked him.

"It's a group in Lisbon that paid Guterres money, from an oil company that I'm going to say had business in Xinjiang," Long said.

Gul nodded. "We do have natural gas," she said. "It's one of the reasons Xi moved all the Han Chinese in."

When the suited man returned, he did let them in - escorted of course. It was to see the lawyer de Souza but rather the new Chief of Staff Rattray. Kurt had prepared Long for this, too. Rattray had been photographed at UN sleazefests hosted by a man who ran so-called modeling agencies, code name for a UN escort service. Some were underage, another connection to the Jeffrey Epstein world of UNSC President Mona Juul.

Up on the 38th floor Rattray stood stiff. "I asked the spokesman," he said, "and he said the only questions he's received about this Gulbenkian Foundation come from a now discredited correspondent. Is this related to him?"

"No it's about genocide," Long said flatly. He turned the floor over to Gul and looked out the window, back toward Grand Central and the tall building he knew that Norway's Mission was housed in, on the 35th floor. That might be their next stop, after this stiff gargoyle. The UN couldn't even do repression right - a totally bush league operation. #GenocideGamesofGuterres.

* * * *

Sometimes you had to have priorities. Or sometimes priorities chose you. Kurt had been live tweeting not only the Sarah Palin versus New York Times trial but also the sentencing of Paul Manafort's lender Stephen Calk's post-trial sentencing when he got the text messages from Michael Randall Long from the UN.

Kurt didn't know Rattray as well he'd known Guterres' previous chief of staff, the former Brazil Ambassador who after a dignified anti-Western diplomatic turn during the UN votes on bombing Libya (they gave the US the green light) had helped Guterres cover up dozens of child rapes.

Once after he was thrown out of the UN and was biking down Second Avenue to the public library where he set up shop to continue covering the UN Kurt had seen her crossing the street and turned around. "You know they are not even answering my written questions," Kurt had said, and then yelled.

The Brazilian lady looked scared and quickened her step in the snowy streets. It made Kurt wonder what he was doing, what he had become. Her name was Maria Luiza Ribeiro Viotti.

It was easier to hate Courtenay Rattray, a tall sneering get-over who went to whore-monger's parties. For a time he had led the anti-gay caucus in the UN - there is one - and was rewarded by Guterres with a job atop some useless Least Developed Nation bureaucracy. Now he had become Guterres' replacement hatchet man, still block Kurt on Twitter. So Kurt headed north.

Unlike Michael Randall Long and Gul, Kurt didn't take the subway. Too many track fires, too many delays. He took a CitiBike from Foley Square, straight up Centre Street to Canal, then east to Christie, alongside what he called Sarah D. Roosevelt Broken Glass Park. There had been a time he had sat in this park with his teeth throbbing when a filling fell out, drinking for a 40 ounce Olde English and munching Bon Ton potato chips, now Utz.

Now Kurt too had changed, a more serious person, perhaps, more focused, also more bitter he had to recognize. He had come to hate Guterres, the man who had thrown him out of the UN, a beat he had become so used to over the course of a decade. That Guterres was now opening supporting genocide brought it all today. Kurt picked up the pace, feeling his breath grow shorter as he approached the UN on First Avenue, past the Chinese consulate. He had come to hate them, too. Li Baodong had helped him, with scoops about Ivory Coast and the right back of beefy Gbagbo. The new Ambassador was just a stone faced ideologue, one who blocked Kurt on Twitter to boot.

Kurt parked his CitiBike on the rack on 44th Street and through of getting a felafel, he hadn't been to this outdoor food truck in some time. But Long had texted him again, and Kurt stopped to reply with more dirt, more code words, more fodder to get Long and Gul deeper into the sanctuary of sleaze. Since Kurt knew from hard won knowledge he was on the blacklist, he decided to branch out.

Norway's Mission to the UN is in the One Dag, an official building that had also housed the scam South South News funded by CCP bribed Ng Lap Seng. A dozen played out Ambassadors had been given office there, to lobby the UN for various things for China. A construction contract for a supposed convention center cum casino in Macau, and probably these Olympics, indirectly.

The SDNY prosecutors had scratched the surface of Macau, putting Ng in jail after a trial that Kurt had covered everyday in the same courtroom that Calk was being sentenced in today, back when Kurt could still bike back to the UN before 7 pm and get in, to write up his articles in the media bullpen on the fourth floor. Where had all those Periscope videos gone?

Kurt knew what to say to get past the guards at One Dag. If you mentioned one of the many diplomatic missions in the building, they would stop you and call upstairs. If you said you were visiting the derivative NGO Security Council Watch, they waved you through. Who would be going to shoot that place up? There was, of course, a temperature check. But Kurt passed it with flying colors. And soon he was on the express elevator up to the 35th door.

"I'm here to see Mona Juul," Kurt told the Norwegians' guard.

"She is at the Security Council," was the reply. And then what Kurt had expected, "Do you have any appointment?"

"The Security Council is not meeting right now," Kurt continued, dodging the second part.

"Yes but as president she must be there, having meetings."

Kurt saw another Mission staffer he knew, one who shuttled back and forth working for the UN. He said her name - not included here - and this got in into the waiting room.

A dozen Mission staffer, ten of them blonde, were watching the NBC feed of the Olympics on a big screen TV and cheering. Norway was racking up the medals, and China was not calling re-play and disqualifying them as it had with the Americans.

Norway knew when to shut up and dribble, or cross country ski as the case may be. Through Terje Roed Larsen they had done it in Kazakhstan; as Kurt had exposed while still in the UN, they had done it to steal Somalia's oil. Very environmental. A welfare state funded by offshore crude oil, virtue signaling about Carbon Neutrality. They fit together with Guterres and his Genocide Games like a hand in a curling glove.

"There is a Uighur woman inside the UN, trying to meet with Mona Juul," Kurt blurted out. The woman he recognized, and who it seemed recognized him, came over.

"Xinjiang is not on the agenda of the Security Council," she said.

"I wonder why not," Kurt said. He remembered when, in 2009, Turkey had tried to put it on and suffered massive punch back by China. The idea was never even raised again, and wasn't even floated now by the US Mission.

"The Uighur refugee is asking to meet Juul in her capacity as Norway's Ambassador," Kurt said. "And if Juul refuses I'll writing about it."

Some people in UN world still read Kurt's blog, and not only people interested in the SDNY courthouse. It had gone from niche media in Turtle Bay to a niche media in Foley Square, a better beat on balance, but one in pain, like a person with an involuntarily amputated limb.

"And she wants me to attend the meeting," Kurt added. Which wasn't technically true. But that had never stopped him before.

"Then it can't be inside the UN," the woman said. "Let me see if something is possible. But you must leave here now."

"On that basis, yes," Kurt said. "But at the drop of a hat, I can be back."

The woman made a mental note to put Kurt on the blacklist of One Dag, including facial recognition on the temperature checking tablet if Kurt tried to use another name. It was Chinese technology. #GenocideGamesOfGuterres.

* * *

The revolving or revolting door in Guterres' UN had gathered speed.

It was Zampolli with whom Rattray, then Jamaica's Ambassador, was cavorting. Then Rattray got a UN job, and now another as chief of staff.

On the morning of February 10, Inner City Press tweeted a first photo of Rattray with Guterres and a long time UN ambassador and official; one was charged with domestic sexual abuse, more on which on this platform going forward.

The Norwegian staffer Meena Syed, the other hand, has been placed as a mole in the Office of the President of the General Assembly, in which she witnessed pro-China corruption she never reported on except perhaps to her Norwegian bosses. They used this info for their own benefit with China, *perhaps for the country's sovereign wealth fund's murky oil business, perhaps for more personal lucre, like Juul and Roed-Larsen's $130,000 from Jeffrey Epstein.*

The Brazilian lady Maria Luiza Ribeiro Viotti would surely resurface, if she wanted to. The former spokesman Martin Nesirky was now at the UN in Vienna, where he intervened to block Kurt from even an online press briefing. Once the UN corrupted you, you never really left. Tony Banbury had appeared to be the exception, with a gentle critique in the gray lady now being sued by Sarah Palin. But that was only in order to work for tech billionaire deeply corrupted by China. So all roads led to the post-modern Rome. #GenocideGamesOfGuterres.

* * *

When Kurt came out of One Dag he had an idea. He'd seen the Chinese dissident artist's posters, depicting athletes stopping to shoot a Uighur, and snowboarding on top of surveillance cameras like the bannisters skateboarders went down.

Kurt texted Martin Randall Long. "R u still in UN?"

"Yes," Long replied. "& we're supposed to come back in the afternoon. Run-around I'm sure."

"Print out those posters and take a few back in. Let's see what the UN does." Kurt knew, of course. Before he was thrown out, he'd posted on the inside glass door of the office he and Brazilian photographer Luiz shared the sign of a group they started, FUNCA, the Free UN Coalition for Access.

Soon enough a UN "Media Accreditation and Liaison" staffer, Chinese no less but any other nationality in the UN would have done it including American, told Kurt that if he didn't take the poster down, he would be thrown out. He had kept it up, until one day he came back to his supposed locked office and found it gone. They had the key. To his computer as well, probably. It was the beginning of the end. #GenocideGamesOfGuterres.

* * *

Michael Randall Long was aware of the ways that a censor could block a poster. An organization could say, Post no bills, an old world for anything affixed to a wall. But while an organization could say, no T-shirts with messages, could it really distinguish between types of messages, at least if they did not contain pornography?

Inside the UN, people not only bought and worse UNICEF t-shirt, they also had others with saccharine slogans like "Every Woman, Every Child." (To the UN Peacekeepers, that seemed to mean, rape or abuse EWEC).

So Long and Gul put on their Badiucao shirts when they went back in - or after they got in, to be more precise. Down in the basement of the General Assembly, where the UN hawked world peace shot glasses and golf tees, there was a public bathroom, that Kurt had used in the past to change into his blue Oxford cloth shirt before going to the UN noon briefings.

Inside, in the Men's and Women's bathrooms -- no UNisex in the UN -- Michael Randall Long and Gul each put on a Badiucao shirt, then met back out by the soda and potato chip vending machines. They went back up the spiral staircase to General Assembly lobby.

But they didn't get far.

One UN guard pointed them out, and spoke into a walkie-talking. Soon six guards appeared, led by a seventh in a white shirt.

"You know you can't wear that here," the officer announced.

"Where what here?" Long replied.

"The shirt. I'm going to have to ask you to take it off, or to leave."

Gul cut in. "But we paid twenty dollars to be here. Each."

"There are rules in this Organization," the officer said.

"What, rules to protect China for criticism?" Gul asked.

As the guards looked at each other, Long added in, "Or to protect Fat Tony Guterres?"

The officer in the white shirt shook his head and said to the others, "Take them out."

Gul was getting into this, figuring they couldn't just do it like China. "What, take us out like kill us?"

Two guards grabbed her, one on each arm. Four more had come over, in thick bullet proof jackets marked ESU. One of the flashed an automatic weapon, what looked like an Uzi.

"You're going to shoot us?" Gul demanded. Other tourists stared over, most of them moving away. Nothing to see here.

Long decided to play lawyer. "What is your name?" he demanded from the white shirted guard.

"You don't have to tell them," White Shirt said to the others. They were already being pushed out through the silver revolving doors with the relief sculptures of peace scenes. There was some other art work on the plaza but Martin Randall Long didn't have time to see it, they were pushing him so fast.

"My name, by the way, is Ronald Dobbins," the guard said. "Roland E. Dobbins." #GenocideGamesOfGuterres.

* * *

There was a protest, albeit a small one, headlined by a Long Island politician in the Dag Hammarskjold Park, surrounded by police. Some of the protesters wore the powder blue masks that had come to symbolize the Uighur issue. Kurt, on his way out from and already banned from One Dag, pulled out his phone and was about to start streaming, or trying to stream, when across First

Avenue he saw a commotion, and a person he recognized.

It was Michael Randall Long, being pushed out of the UN by a guard whom Kurt also recognized. Kurt ran across the Avenue, past a bronze statue of a man with a briefcase, a symbol of UN corporate inaction perhaps, and yelled, trying to get Dobbins to stay outside the gate so he could film him. Again.

Dobbins looked up and smiled. "I told you," he said loudly to Kurt. "I told you that you would never get back in."

Actually Kurt had been coming to think it might be best to do this fight from outside, without having to make compromises just to be able to sit once a day surrounded by complicit careerists a/k/a correspondents and feel good asking questions that the UN never answered. That was a US State Department move.

"F*ck you, Dobbins," Kurt yelled, free. "One day you'll get your Nuremburg. Maybe."

These comparisons weren't helpful, and were one of the things that kept Kurt from the Long Island protest in the park. But whatever. Kurt jogged across the little plaza with benches in front of the

UN's Visitors' Entrance. He said to Gul, "Are you alright?"

"My parents are in worse shape," Gul replied. "But what do we do now?"

Kurt thought of interviewing her, right here, for his vlog. But maybe he should call other, so called "real," media. Would the guys at Fox come and cover this, as one of them had the time that he was first barred entry here, on July 5, 2018? They were reporting mostly on Biden's incoherent immigration policies now.

Kurt was searching his phone for the Foxites' number or email address (he mostly communicated with them, one way, by tagging one of them in photos on Twitter) when a van pulled up in the red-painted bus lane and a half dozen men got out.

They came over and got right to the point. They grabbed Michael Randall Long by the t-shirt, tearing it, and pushed him to the ground.

"What the f*ck" Kurt started to say - the UN guards including Dobbins had ripped his shirt, too, back on July 3, 2018 -- when two of the men came over him. One grabbed his phone.

"This is America!" Kurt yelled dramatically.

"Not here," one of the men said. And through the UN Gate, Kurt saw Dobbins watching, and laughing.

"Whycha call Eric Adams," Dobbins shouted through the gate. "This is international territory. And we of the same mind." #GenocideGamesOfGuterres.

* * *

There was protest outside the UN during the Olympic, which got almost no coverage. Eric Adams, views on Uighurs unknown, was said by Politico to be running the city from a fancy restaurant in midtown, flanked by a previously convicted fraudster. His issue was the rising crime rate and maybe, though backsliding, crypto.

The NYPD's policy as to the area outside the UN gate, but before the First Avenue, curb remain unclear. Inner City Press did a FOIL request, which the NYPD delayed on and never substantively answered. Attempts to get other media interested went nowhere. A guy from a wire service kept saying he might write about it, but there was always another new crime they covered, still most of them Orange hued.

The blue masks are surely authentic, but also seemed to dehumanize the victims. Maybe it was just Kurt. Genocide Games of Guterres.

* * *

"I say we go to the police precinct," Michael Randall Long said. "The only way we can sue, if we can, is if we build a paper trail."

"I just want to get my phone back," Kurt said.

"Mine too," Gul said softly. They hadn't seen, but during the hoopla, the men from the van had taken her Metro PCS phone. We're lucky they didn't take her, Long thought. What a fiasco. How would he keep up with his other cases down at SDNY, and over at EDNY in Brooklyn?

Kurt despite his bluster had much the same thought. He was supposed to be covering the end game of Sarah Palin versus New York Times, said to be a seminal First Amendment case, down to the nitty gritty of whether or not James Bennet had clicked of link to a story that contradicted his assumptions about Sarah Palin, or "blood libel" as she'd called it.

James Bennet of course was a good friend of Alison Smale, an arrogant New York Times-er who once she got a job at the UN worked to get Kurt banned, proud when right media published a story naming her. The only other online site that even mentioned her were either her own UN News propaganda, or Kurt's then public library posts, replete with misspellings. Now she was back in Europe.

Probably defending the Olympic "ideal" against the boycotts, Kurt thought. He still had a Google Alert for her names but the hits were fewer and fewer.

Long, Kurt and Gul walked west to the 17th Precinct, through Dag Hammarskjold Park where homeless people had replaced the Genocide Games protesters, and up Second Avenue under the shadow of One Dag and past the luxury condo building where Norway kept a penthouse Kurt had been invited to once, to hear spin about that royal family's visit to that year's UN General Assembly week, before he was thrown out.

Turned out the Norway royal family, like their non-royal Ambassador Mona Juul, had a connection with pedophile Jeffrey Epstein. Princess Mette-Marit has cavorted with Epstein, just like

Miss Sweden Eva Andersson Dubin, then claimed she hadn't known what he was up to. Totally corrupt, and now running the Security Council, silent on the Genocide Games.

At the precinct they made the three of them wait in the ticky tacky entrance, filling out a form that said "Incident" at the top. Finally a Sergeant came out and looked at the form. "It happened on international territory," he said. "Don't think there's much we can do about it."

"But it was outside the UN gate," Long said.

"We start at the curb onto First Avenue," the sergeant said.

"Where is that written down?" Long asked.

The sergeant looked at him, and rolled together his lips as if he were using Chapstick. "I'll take the form," he finally said. "I just wouldn't expect much from it."

Kurt had been deferring to Michael Randall Long, Gul's lawyer, but now spoke up. "And what about my phone?"

"You put it in the incident report," the sergeant said. "But I'd think about getting another one."

Kurt, now getting journalistic or zeitgiesty again, had a question. "Are you guys watching the Winter Olympics here?"

The sergeant laughed. "Buncha cheaters and curling? Nah," he said.

"Because of the Uigoors?" Gul asked.

"The what?" the sergeant asked.

Gul had lit up, looking more interested. "China's human rights record."

"Maybe," the cop said. "Mostly, it's on at the wrong times" He paused then said, "Go Bengals!" Genocide Games of Guterres.

* * *

Kurt did stop and get a new phone, at the T-Mobile story on 45th and Third Avenue. Now he was glad he hadn't figured out how to discontinued the predatory insurance and tech support contract. He got another Samsung flip phone and spend an hour in the freezing second floor eating area of the Korean deli across Third Avenue using the City's Wi-Fi to re-download his apps. Maybe this way he could get back into streaming, opening up a small space in the media miasma that was the second and final week of the Genocide Olympics. #Genocide Games of Guterres.

It's true that the 17th precinct does want to take any complaints about that UN. It happened on July 4, 2018, and subsequent FOIL requests led nowhere. And it's true that without paperwork including medical visits, most lawyers won't even consider suing a diplomatic mission much less the UN. Even a big pro bono firm, for now unnamed, that said it would, hasn't. The international legal system is broken, with a big blind spot at the center: Big Tony.

The cheating had only begun, in the first week of the genocide games. A skater pushed to the ice, another allowed to practice then compete despite a positive drug test. Was it all a precursor to an invasion of Ukraine? Genocide Games of Guterres.

Kurt had kept his hand in fighting redlining banks and other financial companies; he wrote blogs about how the Administration's promise to crack down was, like so many of its promises (as on the diplomatic boycott) more bark than bite.

But Kurt noticed that VISA, the massive credit card and payments company, was all in with the

Genocide Games. They were the only non-Chinese method to finance at the Games. When asked, ever so gently, about this blood money, they bragged about financial inclusion. Like so many US based banks. (Kurt was also gearing up for the Fed's shadow boxing virtual public hearing on US Bancorp and Mitsubishi United Financial Group, but that's another story).

VISA also partnered with the UN Federal Credit Union, with its headquarters in Long Island City, Queens. So Kurt took the 7 train from Grand Central, snaking out by the new condo towers that had replaced Five Pointz, past Court Square named for a now-dormant courthouse and into Queensboro Plaza.

There were not protests in front of the UNFCU, which was also the payment vehicle for an indicted Iranian spy name Afrasiabi. But now Kurt had his new new phone and was live streaming again. At least he tried. He ranted for two minutes and twenty seconds, about Xinjiang and Guterres and Michele Bachelet, leaving out the part about Afrasiabi. Then he found that the stream could not be replayed, and neither could it be turned into a YouTube video. Time for a new platform. #GenocideGamesOfGuterres.

Kurt decided to walk back under the train tracks to Vernon Jackson. At the condo towers he saw a door open, under a fake Banksi, and went in. The basketball court on the second floor was open, with a half deflated basketball at mid-court. He picked it up and heaved it to the basket on the far end. Why was basketball, played in the winter in the US, not on the Winter Games? And why was Enes Kanter Freedom now not only off NBC but out of the NBA? #GenocideGamesOfGuterres

UNFCU is supposed to comply with US sanctions but doesn't. It paid a spy for Iran's mission; it defraud UN local staff in Sudan on the dollar exchange rate. Now the UN was trying to slip dollars to the Taliban, with an inflated exchange rate like they gave the Burma junta and Zimbabwe, back in the day (before Kurt and Inner City Press were banned from the UN for exposing it).

The destruction of Five Pointz and replacement by ghoulish faux Banksi and swimming pools for the rich like the Bitfinex hackers said it all about New York City, under supposed progressive Bill De Blasio and authentic pescatarian Eric Adams. And no, their door was never open.

* * *

The repercussions of the seizure of Gul's if not yet Kurt's phone were already been sold. Gul told Michael Randall Long that people in her WhatsApp and Telegram chat groups were now being detained in Xinjiang, some reappearing in the concentration camps, some still not resurfacing. (Maybe in the river when the winter was over, Gul added.)

"We have to sue," Gul said. "And I want to sue the UN."

Since Gul lived in Flushing, Queens, and for other reasons, Michael Randall Long decided that if they sued it would be in the Eastern District courthouse in Cadman Plaza in Brooklyn. And it would be better to try to at least file the suit before the Genocide Games were over. But was there time?

Already NBC, which had devoted all of Sunday to predicting that the LA Rams would win, then celebrating when it happened, was gushing about the six gold medals the supposedly boycotting Americans had won so far. Administration defenders reminded that it was a diplomatic boycott, pressure brought to bear by the US government not going, while the athletes could compete.

But from the White House and Foggy Bottom China was scarcely mentioned. It was all, Russia is going to invade Ukraine. Russia is going to invade Ukraine. And from the margins of the podcast world, the hipster duo Kurt had met in 40 Foley of SDNY during the Ghislaine Maxwell trial were mocking the call to war, blaming the West in way that surprise even Kurt, reminding him of played out Soviet spy-wannabes he's met in the UN before he was thrown out.

Michael Randall Long was going to need help with the papers. He sometimes worked with a law student clinic at Fordham Law School up by Columbus Circle but this was too short a turn around for them. He knew a Fordham Law School grad, quite well: Kurt. But would he cross the fourth wall and help with a case rather than just cover it? GenocideGamesOfGuterres.

TrueAnon is a funny podcast, with a "Jeffrey Epstein!" theme song, that thrives on this same platform. Kurt got to know the two creators, and perhaps the sound engineer, in the hallway outside the overflow courtroom for US v. Maxwell in December 2021. Now they were talking Bandera and Nazis and Ukraine, mocking Victoria Nuland as Kurt once had, during the Maidan shooting spree. ("Who Called the Shots," had been his headline).

And yes, Kurt had gone to Fordham Law School, at night, most late afternoon taking the so called Ram Van from Rose Hill down through the traffic of the West Side Highway. It had given him free access to Lexis-Nexis which he had obsessively used and still missed, a minor missing limb like the UN was a larger limb for him. He'd been listed as a member of the SDNY bar by a judge in the Avenatti case(s). But to file a case in EDNY, even co-file? He's have to go over there. #GenocideGamesOfGuterres.

* * *

So Kurt and Gul and Michael Randall Long took the 4 train from Foley Square the four stops to Brooklyn's Borough Hall, then the walk to the Federal courthouse. They had to have their temperatures taken at the entrance, and to give up their phones at the metal detector. (Kurt made a note to apply for a press pass here, like he had at SDNY - then he could bring his laptop and cover the cases here, like the current US v. Jho Lo and Roger Ng of Goldman Sachs, about 1 Malaysia Development Bank).

To file their case they had to go to the Clerk of Court, but it didn't reopen until 2 pm, and then only until 3. Kurt went up to the sixth floor to the media overflow room for US v. Ng, where some twenty reporters sat taking notes as a party planner described how they had bought Leo DiCarprio and Jaimie Foxx and had "wrangled models," whatever that met. (Ng's lawyer asked on cross).

At 2 pm they got in line, behind a pro se guy and another long ago defendant who asked for a transcript of his own allocution, only to be told that it was sealed. Finally they moved up to the window and filed their lawsuit and paid the fee. American Express was not accepted, so Michael Randall Long had to use his personal bank card. F*ck it. He believed in this case. #GenocideGamesOfGuterres

* * *

The clerk, after a Long look at the papers, said "You're gonna have to wait, I have to ask for approval to file them."

Michael Randall Long nodded. Kurt noticed that Long didn't demand to know why, as he would have.

"Because of the request for emergency relief," the clerk continued. "I have to see if we wheel it out to Magistrate on that."

"Got it," Long said, smiling. Kurt thought, maybe his approach is more effective.

When the three got out of the clerk's office, Long said, "Let go up the Mag Court, then, to see how it's working while we wait. In case we have to appear there." Kurt liked to hear that, We.

The door was closed but the Mag Court was open. Unlike in SDNY it was windowless. But it had the same rhythm, of the Magistrate's courtroom deputy bustling around a sheaf of papers, talking the Marshals about "producing" a defendant, making sure the Federal Defender or CJA lawyer was in place. Long apparently knew the one on duty. He nodded back and forth with the guy, who came over.

"I heard your on some case against China," the guy said.

"Word travels fast," Long said.

"A river runs through it," the guy continued. "Your timing could be good, with the Olympics and all. But you're gonna have problems with immunity."

"I know," Long said. "Any ideas."

"Lemme ask around," the guy said. "But first, lemme plead my client not guilty."

"Of course," Long said. He, Kurt and Gul settled in for the show. It was like being in church. GenocideGamesOfGuterres.

bonus

EDNY is colder and more formal then SDNY, even the contemporaneous 500 Pearl. Maybe it only seemed that way to Kurt. He had come to know all of the Court Security Officers and most of the Marsals in SDNY. Here they looked at him suspiciously, or just like any other defendant or journalist or pro hace vice lawyer, whatever. Kurt wanted to get a press pass here, having heard they run for life without any need to renew. But he had to start somewhere. He'd start with Roger Ng. But even on that they made him wait.

Kurt had already taken to criticizing some of the judges in EDNY online, on Google News, something he didn't do at SDNY. There was Ann Donnelly, who had ruled no press in the courtroom for the R.Kelly trial which he had covered. Judge Garaufus had ruled against him, no call-in line for the NXIVM sentencings.

Now Chief Judge Margo Brodie, no press in the courtroom for Roger Ng and Tim Leissner, and the still missing Jho Lo. Still somehow Kurt liked the EDNY. It could be his fal- back, his safety valve, if anything fell apart at SDNY as had for him at the UN. China had helped get him thrown out of the UN. Would he get him or this case thrown out of the US courts? #GenocideGamesOfGuterres.

* * *

Kurt was in the Jho Lo trial minus Jho Lo, listening to Tim Leissner brag about bribes and becoming a hero at Goldman Sachs by ripping off the people of Malaysia when Michael Randall Long stuck his head into the overflow courtroom, along with a Court Security Officer. Both gestured for Kurt to come out into the hall.

This getting the hook made Kurt anxious. He'd faced it nearly daily at the UN near the end, and already a few times at SDNY. But he got up, nodded goodbye to a wire service journalist who'd listened but never done anything about his ouster by the UN, and went out.

"What is it?" he asked Long.

"I called a colleague who knows EDNY inside and outside," Long said. "He predicted we can't get any action directly on China, at least not in the time frame we need it. But he gave me an idea."

"What?"

"There's this case here about an NYPD officer who was caught spying for the Chinese Mission to the UN. He said there's a lot of filings sealed in it and we could seek to intervene on an emergency basis."

Kurt nodded. "But if the judge on the case has already allowed the sealing, why is he going to act for us, at least quickly?"

"That's the idea," Long said, seeming pleased at Kurt's issue-spotting. "That judge is away this week. So we could make an emergency application to the Part 1 judge. But it should be from a journalist, not just a lawyer. That's where you come in."

Great, Kurt thought. Another test case, right when he was thinking of trying to get a press pass here, maybe even a little desk space in the the Media Room just in case.

"Let's do it," he said. And they started writing the papers right then and there.

* * *

The EDNY Judge they got, Kurt didn't have much faith. It was the same judge who'd banned him and the rest of the press from being in the courtroom for the R.Kelly trial, like they were being banned from being directly in the Roger Ng / Jho Lo trial now. But Michael Randall Long filed the papers, and they got the hearing they asked for.

Judge Donnelly was behind solid plastic barriers that looked like bullet proof protection shields, weird since you couldn't bring even your phone into the courtroom. It was light brown wood and ceilings that seemed higher than in the SDNY.

"So what is this emergency" - she raised her eyebrows - "application? Mister Long?"

"My client Kurt Wheelock seeks to intervene in the Angwang matter and gain access to documents that bear on the Chinese government's penetration of NYPD and other law enforcement in this country."

"I've seen Mr. Wheelock's song about the my R.Kelly trial." The judge smirked. "He seems to have no problem coming up with material."

"It's that he's covering the case of a Uighur refugee who only yesterday, on the sidewalk right outside the United Nations, had her cell phone grabbed by security guards. Since then her relatives and friends in Xinjiang have been detained over there, some even disappeared."

"Sounds like more than a case of, uh, journalism." The judge paused. "Especially musical journalism, if you can call it that."

"We are going to take other steps as well," Long said. Though he didn't know what those might be.

"And this Uighur refugee, why are they not on the caption of your application? They seem like the real party in interest here."

"We can amend," Long said quickly. Although since Gul had set out on the 7 train for Flushing to get her documents out of her apartment she had gone missing. Even her temporary burning phone had stopped answering or pinging. #GenocideGames of Guterres.

* * *

And so with another abduction, along bit of UN impunity and US and NYC negligence, this chapter came to a close, with Kurt Wheelock and Michael Randall Long pursing the issue now in the Eastern District of New York, where Kurt turned to the Jho Low trial, and in the DDC, where he pursued the January 6 cases, and the Bitfinex hack money laundering case of Ilya Lichtenstein and Heather Morgan. The UN of Antonio Guterres refused to answer on any of these, nor on Guterres' shameful visit to the Genocide Games. But Kurt would not cease. #GenocideGamesofGuterres.

www.ingramcontent.com/pod-product-compliance
Lightning Source LLC
LaVergne TN
LVHW050326160826
845677LV00014B/3548

* 9 7 9 8 4 1 9 4 8 3 6 2 0 *